To David and to Lucy
with love

First United States Edition 1991

All rights reserved. No part of this book may be reproduced or transmitted
in any form or by any means, electronic or mechanical, including photocopying,
recording, or by any information storage and retrieval system, without
permission in writing from the Publisher.

Margaret K. McElderry Books
Macmillan Publishing Company
866 Third Avenue
New York, NY 10022

Collier Macmillan Canada, Inc.
1200 Eglinton Avenue East
Suite 200
Don Mills, Ontario M3C 3N1

Copyright © 1991 by Simon James

First published by Walker Books, London
Printed in Hong Kong by South China Printing Co. (1988) Ltd.
10 9 8 7 6 5 4
Library of Congress Catalog Card Number: 90-50815
ISBN 0-689-50529-9

Dear Mr. Blueberry

SIMON JAMES

Margaret K. McElderry Books
New York

Maxwell Macmillan International Publishing Group
New York   Oxford   Singapore   Sydney

Dear Mr. Blueberry,
  I love whales very much and
I think I saw one in my pond
today. Please send me some
information on whales, as
I think he might be hurt.

Love
Emily

Dear Emily,

Here are some details about whales. I don't think you'll find it was a whale you saw, because whales don't live in ponds, but in salt water.

Yours sincerely
Your teacher,

Mr. Blueberry

Dear Mr. Blueberry,

I am now putting salt into the pond every day before breakfast and last night I saw my whale smile. I think he is feeling better.

Do you think he might be lost?

Love
Emily

Dear Emily,

   Please don't put any more salt in the pond. I'm sure your parents won't be pleased.

   I'm afraid there can't be a whale in your pond, because whales don't get lost, they always know where they are in the oceans.

      Yours sincerely,

        Mr. Blueberry

Dear Mr. Blueberry,

Tonight I am very happy because I saw my whale jump up and spurt lots of water. He looked blue.

Does this mean he might be a blue whale?

Love
Emily

P.S. What can I feed him with?

Dear Emily,

Blue whales are blue and they eat tiny shrimplike creatures that live in the sea. However, I must tell you that a blue whale is much too big to live in your pond.

Yours sincerely,

Mr. Blueberry

P.S. Perhaps it is a blue goldfish?

Dear Mr. Blueberry,

Last night I read your letter to my whale. Afterward he let me stroke his head. It was very exciting.

I secretly took him some crunched-up cornflakes and bread crumbs. This morning I looked in the pond and they were all gone!

I think I shall call him Arthur. What do you think?

Love
Emily

Dear Emily,

I must point out to you quite forcibly now that in no way could a whale live in your pond. You may not know that whales are migratory, which means they travel great distances each day.

I am sorry to disappoint you.

Yours sincerely,

Mr. Blueberry

Dear Mr. Blueberry,
  Tonight I'm a little sad. Arthur
has gone. I think your letter made
sense to him and he has decided
to be migratory again.

Love
Emily

Dear Emily,

Please don't be too sad, it really was impossible for a whale to live in your pond. Perhaps when you are older you would like to sail the oceans studying and protecting whales.

Yours sincerely,

Mr. Blueberry

Dear Mr. Blueberry,

It's been the happiest day!
I went to the beach and you'll
never guess, but I saw Arthur!
I called to him and he smiled.
I knew it was Arthur because
he let me stroke his head.

I gave him some of my
sandwich . . .

and then we said good-bye.
   I shouted that I loved him very
much and, I hope you don't mind,
I said you loved him, too.

   Love
      Emily (and Arthur)

The End